HOLIDAY COLLECTION

ON CHRISTMAS EVE

ON CHRISTMAS EVE

By Margaret Wise Brown

Illustrated by Beni Montresor

Young Scott Books

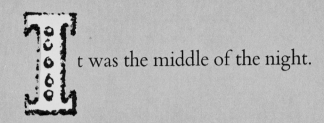It was the middle of the night.

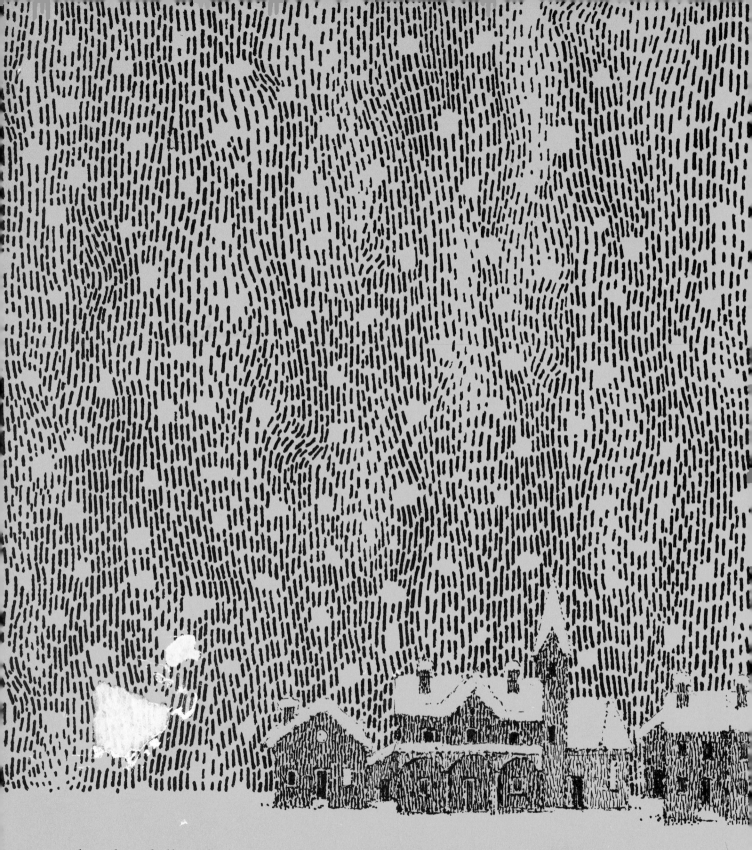

And night of all nights it was Christmas.

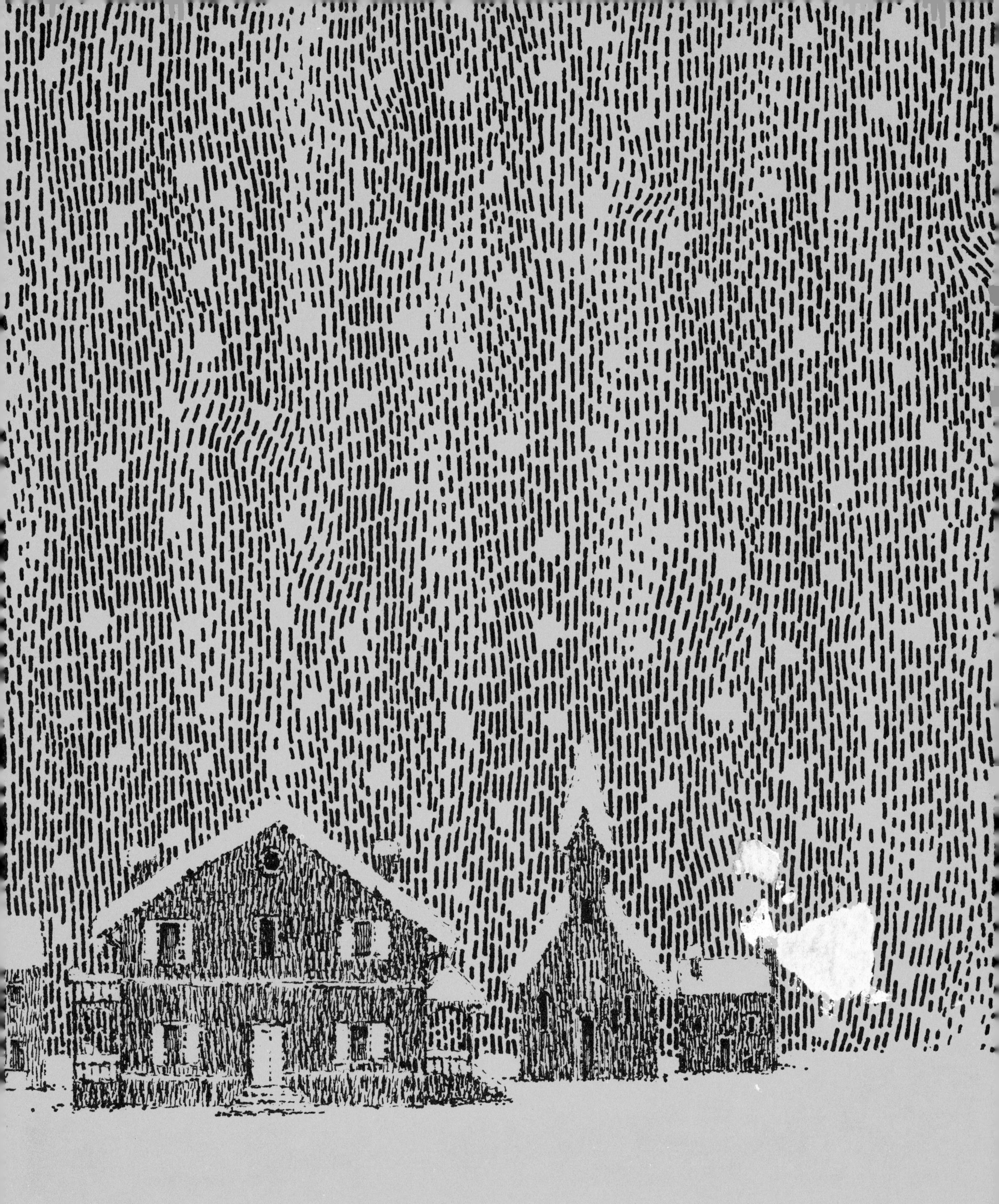

The children couldn't sleep.

They had lain in bed for hours,

listening and pretending.

They saw reindeer and sugar plums
and angels and stars and wise men.

Then one of the children said,

"Let us all go down and touch the tree

and make a wish

before we go to sleep."

So very quietly in the large cold playroom

they took their clothes under the covers

and dressed themselves.

They put on their sweaters and slippers

and socks and bathrobes.

In the big quiet house

where the people were sleeping,

the children got out of their beds.

Then into the upstairs hall they went—
quietly, almost without breathing
they went, past the door where Mother
and Father were sleeping. So quietly
through the hall.

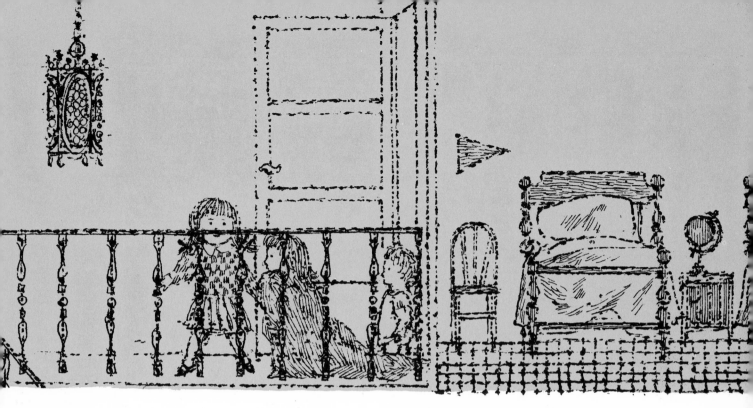

No sound until the top stair creaked.
Then they all stood terribly still
and listened. No sound but their
own thumping hearts.

And now they were creeping downstairs

in the middle of the night—

night of all nights—Christmas

night.

Out the window it even looked like Christmas.

The quietest night in the world with snow falling

so softly. So quietly.

Great green evergreen branches on the stairs

and red holly berries in the hall.

Downstairs it was still warm. The warm smells of

Christmas, pine trees and wood smoke and oh wonderful

smell of Christmas seals and packages not yet

opened. The night before Christmas, Christmas Eve.

Quietly listening, listening all over, with eyes and

ears and hands and feet they went down into the

warm dark pine scented hall.

They came to the living-room door. They listened.

Beyond the windowpane, white flakes

in the blue night, the snow fell down. They couldn't hear it.

A piece of wood creaked in the dying fire.

Then the children went into the room

and stood close together on the soft rug

in front of the fire. They couldn't speak or move.

It was as though a magic had come true.

The Christmas tree was all there,

trimmed with shiny glints of red and blue and green

that flickered in the dying firelight.

Silver and gold tinsel hung all over the tree,

loads and loads of tinsel, gold tinsel.

And, in front of the chimney

where they could reach out and touch them,

hung their stockings filled with little white bundles

and tangerines and strange shapes.

If they reached out their hands they could touch them.

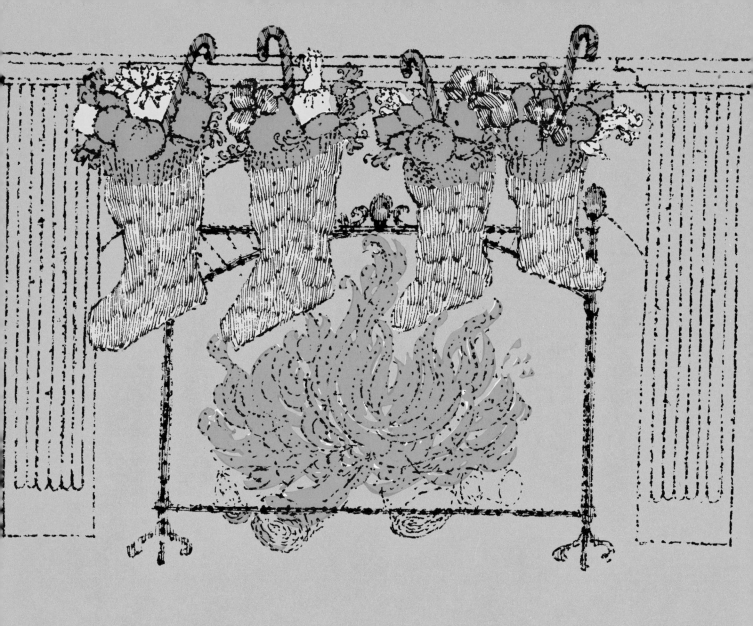

Under the tree were more packages. And there was one

big package. They all saw it. It looked like

an electric train. It went all around the tree.

They all saw it.

No one spoke.

No one moved.

And then suddenly in the night,

through the soft snow falling outside, the voices came.

They really came, those voices,

so quietly in the night, singing:

"Holy Night   Silent Night   All is calm   All is bright"

The children ran to the window.

Dark figures were moving outside in the snow.

The dark figures carried a lantern. They were

grown-up people singing. The children listened.

The sound of the voices

seemed to fall with the snow.

> *"Sleep in heavenly peace*
>
> *Sleep in heavenly peace"*

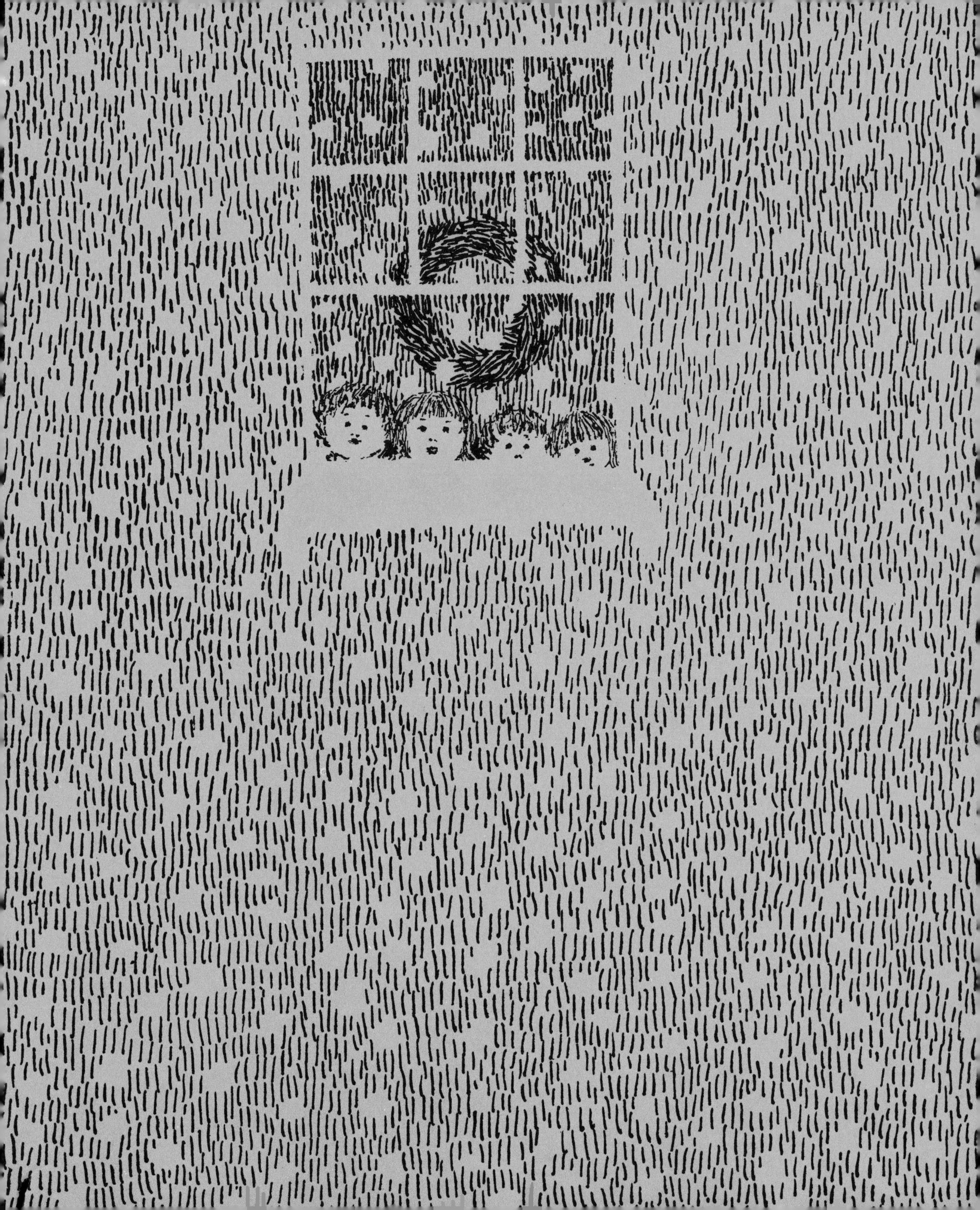

The song stopped. There was

that quietness of snow again. The grown-up people

moved around outside, dark figures

against the white snow.

The Christmas Carolers. They were the Christmas

Carolers, grown-up people who went from house

to house singing Christmas songs

on Christmas Eve.

The children quickly turned toward the stairs.

They went up the stairs almost running, only as quietly still as they could.

And they jumped into bed with their clothes on.

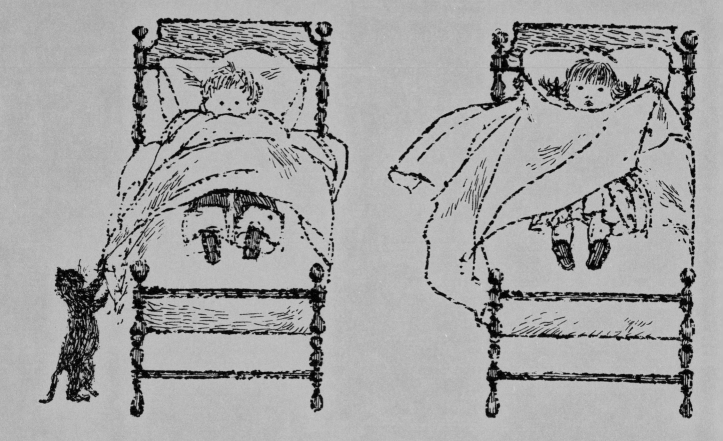

Their hearts were pounding.

Then the singing began again:

"*God rest you merry gentlemen*
Let nothing you dismay
Oh Tidings of Comfort and Joy."

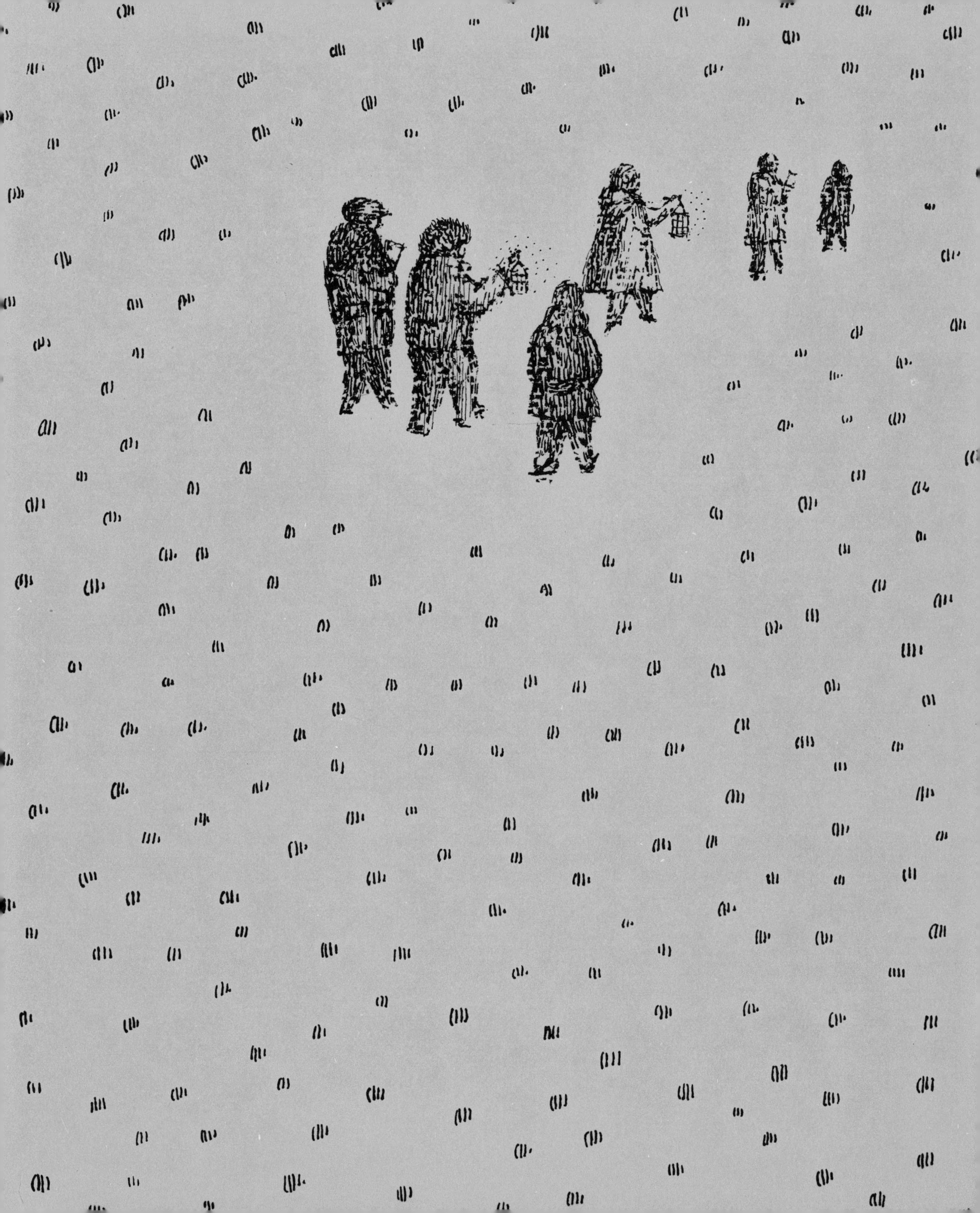